DISCARD

One More Time, Mama

by Sue Alexander

illustrated by David Soman

MARSHALL CAVENDISH   NEW YORK

Text copyright © 1999 by Sue Alexander
Illustrations copyright © 1999 by David Soman
All rights reserved
Marshall Cavendish, 99 White Plains Road,
Tarrytown, NY 10591

Library of Congress Cataloging-in-Publication Data
Alexander, Sue, date
One more time, Mama / by Sue Alexander ;
illustrated by David Soman.
     p.   cm.
Summary: A mother remembers the fireflies, afternoon rain, squirrels, geese, and
other aspects of nature that she watched while waiting for her child to be born.
ISBN 0-7614-5051-3
[1. Nature—Fiction. 2. Mother and child—Fiction.]
I. Soman, David, ill. II. Title.
PZ7.A3784Te 1999 [Fic]—dc21   9847937 CIP AC

The text of this book is set in 16 point Slimbach Medium.
The illustrations are rendered in watercolor.
Printed in Hong Kong
First edition
6 5 4 3 2 1

This book is dedicated with love to my granddaughter
Megan Elizabeth Finn, whose very existence fills me with joy

—S. A.

To Ainslie, Michael, and the
new baby Wallhopper

—D. S.

*L*ook, Mama! The fireflies are dancing over the pond!

I see them, my love.

Tell me again, Mama, about waiting to watch them with me.

Tell me again, one more time.

All right, my love.

My waiting began when the winter winds swirled the snow into drifts and the aspen and tall spruce trees were mirrored in the ice on the pond. By then the bears were bedded down in their forest dens and the snow on the rise was crisscrossed with rabbit tracks.

I could hear the crackle of twigs being broken in the
woods as the deer looked for food and the raspberry bushes
were dressed in frozen dewdrop lace.

But you had to go on waiting,
didn't you, Mama?
    Yes, my love.
    Tell me again about going on waiting.
    All right, my love.

My waiting went on when the thaw began and the bears in their forest dens were beginning to wake. I could hear the ice on the pond snap as it broke into small floes and I could see daffodils begin to push up through patches of melting snow on the rise.

It was soon after that when the first ducks and geese of the season came back to the pond to find cozy spots in the shore grasses to build their nests.

But I wasn't here yet. You still had
to wait, didn't you?

Yes, my love.

Tell me some more about waiting,
Mama. Tell me again.

I was waiting when the new-hatched goslings and ducklings waddled down the path around the pond and the wild violets began to bloom on the rise beyond.

I could hear the sound of crickets echoing
from the trees and the spring showers sent
the starlings flitting under the eaves. It was then
that the blossoms on the cherry trees
looked like tiny puffs of cotton.

But you had more time to wait, didn't you?

Yes, my love.

Tell me again about that time.

I was still waiting when the early-summer sun shimmered on the path and the families of ducks and geese made ripples in the pond as they swam past each other.

I could hear the sound of the woodpeckers
in the trees and smell the wild roses that
grew on the rise.

But I still wasn't here yet. And you had to wait
some more, didn't you, Mama?
Yes, my love.
Tell me what it was like then. Tell me again.

The air was heavy with late-summer heat and the sound of
thunder was never very far away. Sudden bursts of afternoon
rain would spatter the pond, hurrying the ducks and geese
into their nests in the grasses along the shore.

After the rain, I rested in the shade of the willow tree and watched ribbons of butterflies skim over the pond. And then I picked raspberries from the bushes at the edge of the woods.

You were almost done waiting, weren't you, Mama?

Almost, my love.

Tell me again how it was then.

All right, my love.

The fall winds had begun to blow and acorns rat-a-tat-
tatted on the roof as they fell. I watched the squirrels leap
along the path as they scurried to gather them. Apples
were ripe on the trees and maple leaves were beginning
to be edged in scarlet. And it was then, just as the geese
rose up from the pond to start their journey south . . .

That I was here!
Yes, my love.

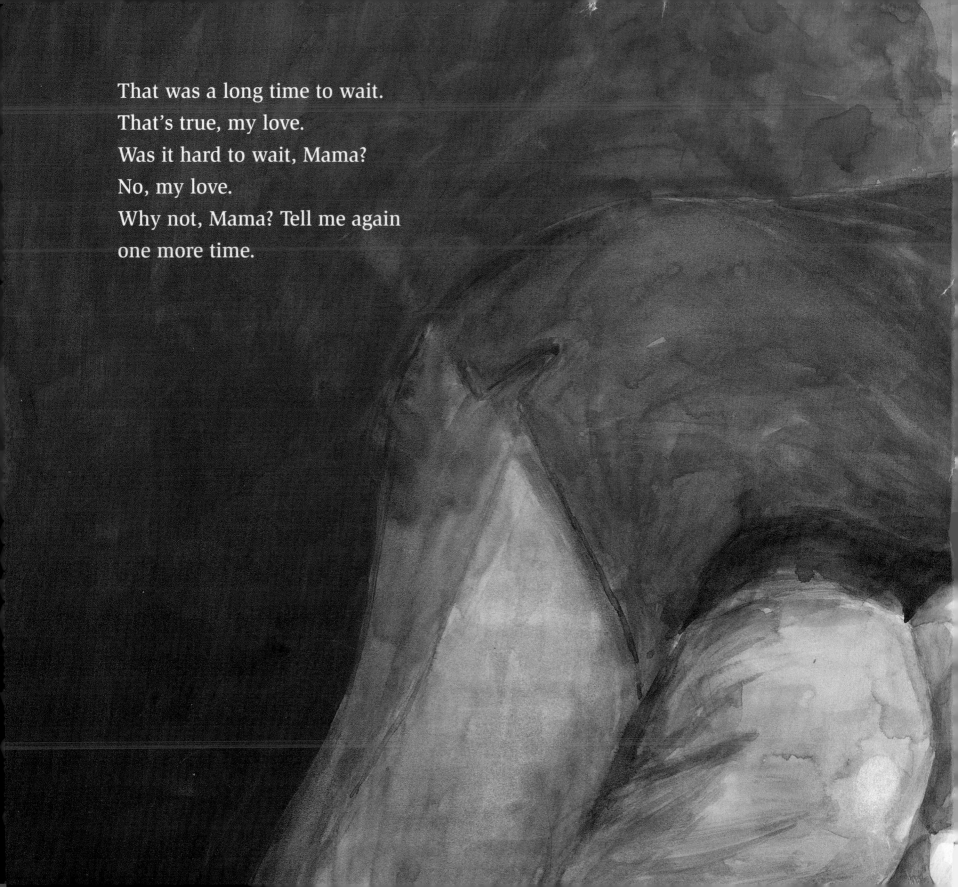

That was a long time to wait.
That's true, my love.
Was it hard to wait, Mama?
No, my love.
Why not, Mama? Tell me again
one more time.

Because, my love, it was you I was waiting for.